LITTLE KAY

◆

ROBIN MULLER

North Winds Press
A Division of Scholastic-TAB Publications Ltd., Richmond Hill, Ontario, Canada

Art Director: Kathryn Cole

87654321   **Printed in Hong Kong**   89/801234/9

Canadian Cataloguing in Publication Data

Muller, Robin
  Little Kay

Issued also in French under title: Puce et le sultan.
ISBN 0-590-71887-8

I. Title.

PS8576.U44L58 1988   jc813'.54   C88-093545-6
PZ7.M84Li 1988

*For Mary Keenan, with gratitude and affection
and in memory of Dandy Burro*

ong ago there lived a magician and his three daughters.

One day a message arrived from the Sultan proclaiming that every noble household must send a son to the palace to serve as knight for a year and a day. This distressed the old magician greatly, for he had no son, and he knew how ill-tempered and unreasonable the Sultan could be.

His daughters sensed their father's unhappiness. "Papa, why do you sigh so?" asked the youngest, whose name was Little Kay. "Have we done something to displease you?"

"No, my dear," he answered. "No one could ask for sweeter children. I am troubled," he said, "because the Sultan has commanded me to send a son to be a knight at his court. If I do not, I will surely be disgraced."

"Never fear," she said boldly. "Change me into a young man with your magic and I will be our family's knight at court."

"Alas, I cannot," sighed her father. "You know my power will not work beyond the boundaries of our land."

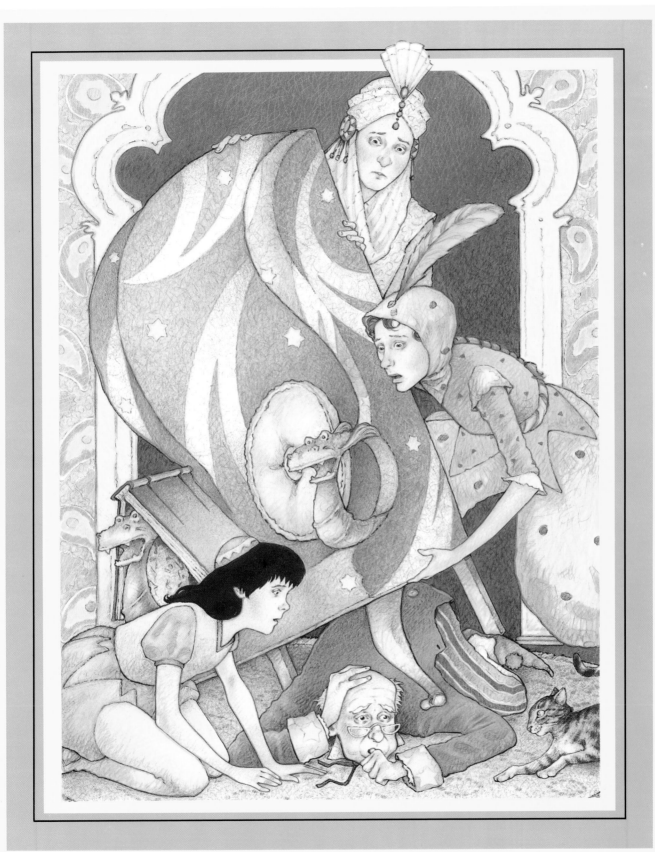

"Then I'll cut my hair short like a man's," cried Little Kay, "and go to the Sultan's court in disguise!"

"A disguise is not enough," protested her father. "You must be brave as well as clever — a true knight. For if the Sultan ever found you out, he would feed you to the savage beasts he keeps as pets."

"I am as brave as any knight," interrupted Morgana, the magician's eldest daughter. "I insist on going. I would rather risk my life than see you in disgrace."

At first the old man refused to consider such a wild scheme, but at last he gave in to her pleas. With her hair cut short, dressed like a mighty warrior, Morgana set out full of confidence.

But the magician was deeply afraid of what might happen to his daughter at the Sultan's court, so he devised a plan to make her turn back. First he changed himself into a crow and flew ahead of her. Then, at the bridge that marked the border of his land, he transformed himself into an enormous lion.

When Morgana reached the bridge the lion sprang out with a terrifying roar, its red jaws fringed with dagger-sharp teeth. Morgana screamed and, forgetting her mission, raced for the safety of home.

Morgana tearfully told her father what had happened. "It's all for the best," he said. "I will accept my disgrace."

"No, you will not," declared Little Kay. "Let me –" But before she could finish, Tamara, the magician's second daughter, spoke up. "I will go as our family's knight," she said. "I am not afraid of a lion's roar."

The old magician tried every argument to dissuade her, but Tamara was adamant. With her hair cut short, armed with sword and shield, she rode out.

Once again the magician flew ahead, and this time changed himself into a ferocious boar. As Tamara approached, the boar rushed out, snorting and tearing the ground in front of her terrified horse. Screaming with fear, she turned her steed and raced back to her father's house.

"That's it!" cried the magician when he heard her tale. "There will be no more nonsense about pretending to be a knight."

"Oh, yes there will, Papa," piped up a fierce voice. Little Kay stood before him with her fists on her hips and her face scrunched into a most ferocious glare. "Now it's my turn!"

"My sweet pomegranate," he laughed, "even if the Sultan wanted to boil me in oil, I wouldn't dream of letting you try. You are far too young and small."

"Papa's right," said her sisters. "Where would we find armour small enough to fit you?"

"I shall make some," cried Little Kay. And she strode from the room.

Little Kay set to work with a hammer and tongs. Soon every room rang with the sound of her banging and clanging. She shaped an old platter and soup pot into armour, a teapot became a helmet, and from the fireplace she chose the largest poker for a lance.

Finally Little Kay went to the stable and took the old donkey that was deaf and nearly blind to be her steed. "Farewell," she shouted. "Look for me this time next year."

"Oh, dear," muttered the old magician sadly, "I'll have to teach her a lesson too. One she'll never forget." And he whispered his spell.

As Little Kay drew near the bridge, the earth suddenly trembled. From a crack in the ground there came an ear-splitting roar and a wall of fire. Out of the flames rose a terrifying dragon, with bulging eyes and gaping jaws.

But Little Kay had prepared herself for a fearsome beast. Digging her heels into the donkey's flanks, she yelled, *"Charge!"* The little donkey, seeing and hearing nothing, galloped forward.

Little Kay dodged between the monster's huge legs, delivered a mighty whack to its rump and, with a leap and clatter, landed on the other side of the river.

Sore and worried, but secretly proud of his daughter, the old magician returned home.

When she arrived at the palace, Little Kay was escorted to the Sultan.

"Well," he sniffed, looking down his long and splendidly curved nose, "what have we here?"

"I am the magician's warrior son, Your Serenity," Little Kay answered proudly. "I have come to serve you for a year and a day."

The Sultan eyed the newcomer suspiciously. Not only was this knight clad in the oddest armour he had ever seen, but he seemed too small and too young to be of any use as a soldier.

"Is this the best the old magician can do?" he mocked. "He might as well have sent me a girl for all the use you'll be!"

He laughed at his own joke, then added with a cruel jeer, "But no one would be stupid enough to send a girl to my court as a knight! Get along to the barracks. We'll soon find out how much of a warrior you are."

As the weeks passed the Sultan saw that Little Kay could indeed ride, joust and swing a scimitar as well as any of the others. But he could not rid himself of the suspicion that all was not what it seemed. Deep in his heart he feared the old magician had tricked him by sending him a girl.

"What a ridiculous thought!" he said to himself. "Girls are not brave and clever as this little knight is. Nevertheless, I'll put him to the test. I will find out if I've been tricked!"

That night he told the cooks to put rings and brooches and necklaces in the porridge that would be served for breakfast the next morning. "If the little knight is a girl, this test will expose her as an imposter," he crowed. "Girls cannot resist pretty things. And woe to the magician if he has tricked me!"

In the barracks the next morning the usual breakfast chatter was broken by shouts of surprise and delight as knight after knight discovered some precious item in his bowl and held it up in wonder. "Look at this!" they said. "How beautiful!" "I love it!" "The Sultan must be pleased with us!" And they put on the jewels and gazed at one another in admiration.

All except Little Kay, who eyed the gifts suspiciously. "Why is the Sultan being so generous?" she wondered as she rubbed the porridge from a diamond clasp. "Here, you have it," she said to a server. "I have no use for such baubles." And she left to practise her archery.

The Sultan was annoyed that his scheme had failed and his suspicions grew darker. Every day the little knight seemed more skilled and more daring, but every day the Sultan grew more certain that he was being tricked.

"It's no use. I must try another test," he decided. "Perhaps some girls don't like jewellery, but no girl can resist draping herself in finery. I will fill the barracks with the most exquisite cloth, slippers and plumes in the kingdom, and then we'll know the truth about the magician's child."

When the knights returned from their javelin lessons, they were amazed to see the barracks filled with bolts of shimmering silk, brocade of woven gold, satin shawls and feathers tinted with the hues of the rainbow.

"The Sultan must be displeased with the way we dress and this is his way of telling us," they cried. Without wasting a moment, they wrapped themselves in the fabulous cloth and twirled about, arranging and rearranging their gorgeous outfits.

All except Little Kay. "Fine feathers don't make a fierce falcon!" she scoffed. "If it's my clothes the Sultan doesn't like, he can tell me to my face." And she left to get her lance sharpened.

Angry that another test had failed, the Sultan paced up and down in his sleeping chamber, scowling at himself in the mirror. Then suddenly his expression changed. "Of course! I know the answer!" he shouted. "The reason the jewels and gowns didn't work is that there were no mirrors to admire them in. No girl in the world can resist a looking glass."

When the knights arose the next morning they found the walls of the barracks brilliant with crystal mirrors. "How marvellous!" they cried, rushing to put on their finery so they could admire their splendid appearance. "We are the most beautiful knights in the world."

"This is really getting ridiculous," giggled Little Kay, gazing at her comrades' antics. "But I suppose boys will be boys." She left for her morning gallop.

With the failure of his latest test, the Sultan was beside himself with fury. "I am being tricked," he bellowed. "I know that I am being tricked. But how can I find out if that little villain is really a man or a maid?"

"That's very easy," said his old housekeeper in surprise. "To tell if a person is a man or not, all you have to do is watch his throat when he drinks. If he's truly a man, his throat will bob like an apple. If it does not, she is most certainly a maid."

That evening the Sultan summoned all his knights to a great banquet. "Stand before me, magician's son," he said slyly to Little Kay. "I have been impressed by your swordsmanship." Then he raised his goblet. "To the knights in my service, brave and true men, every one."

The knights raised their goblets to the toast and downed the wine. Every throat bobbed except Little Kay's. Hers remained as smooth as a marble column.

"Imposter!" the Sultan thundered. "Deceitful wretch! You and your vile family will suffer for this. Fetch me that scheming magician."

"Treacherous brood!" snorted the Sultan when the magician and his daughters were brought before him. "I have in mind a truly horrible punishment for your crime. Would you like to guess what it might be?"

But before anyone could utter a word, the palace shuddered as though hit by an earthquake. The great doors of the chamber burst open and there stood an ogre so huge and so hideous that the Sultan's brave knights fainted at the sight of him.

"I am Jabel," the ogre bellowed, "and today is my birthday! So what do you say?" he roared.

"Happy birthday, Jabel?" whispered the Sultan.

"And what do you do on birthdays?"

"Give presents?" added the Sultan weakly.

"Right!" howled the ogre with a wicked smile. "I have heard you give the most wonderful presents — jewellery and gowns and crystal mirrors. But you forgot to give anything to me!"

"What would you like?" whispered the Sultan.

"For a start I want all your treasure. If everything you have is not in a wagon at the gates in an hour, I will tear this palace down. And then I will squash ten thousand of your subjects like ants under my heel. Just for a start!"

"I am lost!" the Sultan wept when the ogre had gone. "Whatever I give him will never be enough. My kingdom will be destroyed. And not one of my knights is brave enough to stand up to him!"

"I am," piped up a fierce little voice. "I will defeat the ogre!"

"You?" cried the Sultan, gazing in wonder at Little Kay. "Impossible!" He waved at the unconscious knights on the floor. "I certainly can't give you an army."

"I don't need your army," replied Little Kay. "All I need is a small grey plum, a swallow from your battlements, and a leather sack to hold a special surprise. If I tricked someone as wise as you, Your Worriness, surely I can trick a stupid ogre!"

Hastily the Sultan agreed and within the hour a wagon piled high with treasure was at the palace gates.

"Happy birthday to me," roared Jabel. "What a wonderful start! I'll be back when I decide what I want for my next gift!"

As Jabel merrily rode the wagon through the forest, a little figure suddenly sprang out in front of him.

"Halt, ogre, and hand over that treasure — or I'll tear you apart!"

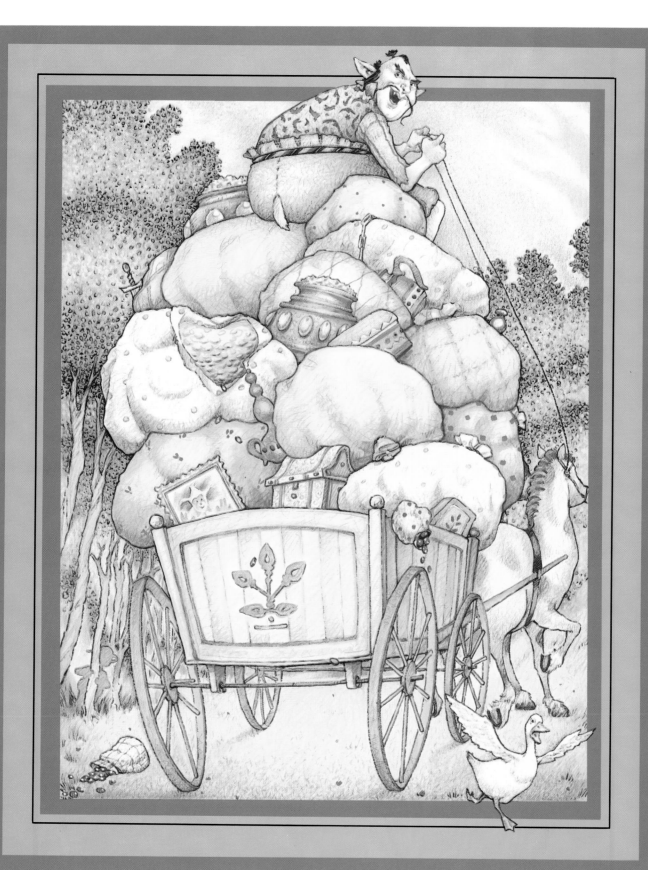

"What?" Jabel squinted down at Little Kay. "Why, you puny little runt! You would need fists of steel to pull me apart."

"That I have," Little Kay proclaimed. "My hands are so strong I can squeeze blood from a stone." Pretending to pick up a rock, she slipped the small grey plum into her hand and squeezed out a stream of sticky red juice.

The ogre stared in surprise, and then he began to snicker. "You can't fool me with that one. That's the old plum trick! Now get out of my way before I throw you over the mountain."

"You mean before I throw you," countered Little Kay. "My arm is so strong that I can fling a stone over the sun." She slipped the swallow into her hand, and with a mighty pitch, hurled the bird into the sky.

The ogre blinked as the dot disappeared into the sunlight, but then he grinned cruelly. "You can't fool me with that one either, you little slug. That was a bird. Out of my way before I skewer you."

But Little Kay stood her ground. She held up the leather sack. "Give me the treasure or my army will fill you with holes."

The ogre roared with laughter. "Now, that's a new one!" He snatched the leather sack.

"Be careful," she warned. "They're asleep and they don't like to be wakened up."

Jabel held the bag to his ear. "I can hear them snoring all right," he sneered, "but I think I'll wake them anyway!" He gave the bag a mighty shake. "Let's see how they like that."

At once a black cloud of hornets swept out of the sack and furiously attacked him. Jabel howled with pain as they stung him again and again. "Brute!" he screamed as he tore through the forest. "Bully!"

Little Kay shook her fist. "And don't come back!" she shouted at the disappearing ogre.

Little Kay marched triumphantly through the palace gates, the treasure in tow. Cheers rose from all sides as she passed, but when she reached the Sultan the crowd grew silent.

The Sultan smiled humbly. "Forgive me, Little Kay," he said. "I was wrong. You have proven yourself both brave and clever, and I appoint you Captain of my Royal Company of Knights." Again the crowd cheered.

"I have decided," he continued, glancing from Little Kay to her father, "that a proclamation shall be issued to every household in the kingdom. From this day forward, daughters as well as sons are welcome to serve at my court!"

The old magician smiled at the Sultan, and Little Kay grinned happily. Together they led the jubilant throng to the magnificent feast that awaited them.

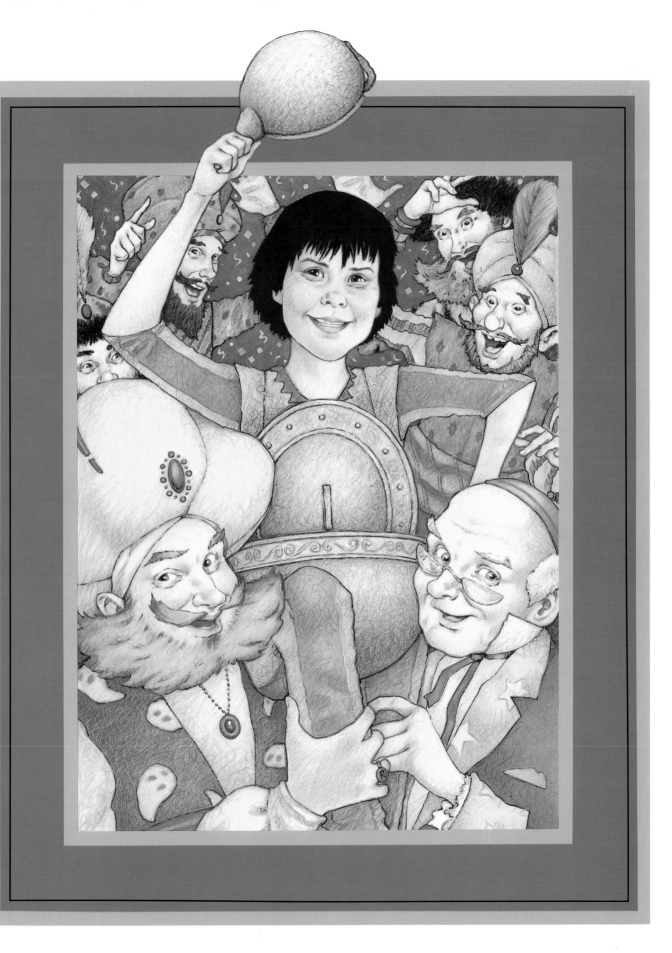